This book belongs to

_____

Disney · PIXAR
WALL·E

A Read-Aloud Storybook

Adapted By
Matthew N. Garret

Illustrated By
Andrea Cagol, Mara Damiani, Caroline Egan, Seung Kim, Maria Elena Naggi, Elizabeth Tate, Scott Tilley, and Giorgio Vallorani

Designed By
Tony Fejeran

Inspired by the art and character designs created by Pixar

Random House 🏠 New York

© 2008 Disney Enterprises, Inc. and Pixar. All rights reserved. Published in the United States by Random House Children's Books, a division of Random House, Inc., New York, and in Canada by Random House of Canada Limited, Toronto, in conjunction with Disney Enterprises, Inc. Random House and colophon are registered trademarks of Random House, Inc. Library of Congress Control Number: 2007939436   ISBN: 978-0-7364-2528-5

www.randomhouse.com/kids/disney

Printed in the United States of America

10 9 8 7 6 5 4 3 2 1

If you had lived during the early twenty-ninth century, you might have been cruising aboard a luxury ship. You might have thought no one was left on Earth. But there *was* someone there, and he had a very important job to do. He was the only one suited for the job, and when he finished it, all the people would be able to return to Earth.

That someone's name was WALL•E (which stood for Waste Allocation Load Lifter, Earth class). WALL•E was a trash-compacting unit whose job was to clean up the polluted planet.

He made the most of it by finding treasures in the trash every day. WALL•E liked his job, but he was very lonely.

On his way home, WALL•E and his pet
cockroach always passed the holo-graphic billboards that
played Buy-n-Large commercials. BnL was the superstore
that had controlled the entire planet. Centuries earlier, it had
made these ads to invite humans to space for vacation-like
cruises. The head of BnL had promised to clean up Earth
while the people were away.

Every night, as WALL•E settled into the trailer he
called home, he put away the treasures he had found
during the day. He also turned on a video of the movie
Hello, Dolly! WALL•E hoped he might one day fall in love
with someone, just like the people in the movie. Then he
wouldn't be lonely anymore.

One day, something different happened—and it changed WALL•E's life forever. It all started when WALL•E found a new kind of treasure that he had never seen before. It was thin and green and very delicate.

"Oooh." WALL•E was filled with wonder. He lifted his beautiful treasure and placed it in an old boot.

Later that evening, WALL•E heard a loud roaring sound coming from the sky. A probe ship landed in a fiery blaze, stirring up a dust storm. Out floated a sleek white robot with bright blue eyes. Her name was EVE. WALL•E fell in love instantly.

WALL•E followed EVE like a puppy dog. He couldn't stay away from her. She appeared to be looking for something.

WALL•E wanted to make friends with EVE, but she seemed wary of strangers. When EVE heard someone behind her, she fired her blaster arm. Luckily, WALL•E was hiding safely behind a boulder.

Finally, EVE seemed to give up on her search. WALL•E approached slowly and showed her how he compacted trash. She told him her job was a secret. Then the two robots introduced themselves.

"Eee-vah," WALL•E repeated, mispronouncing her name.

WALL•E took EVE to his home. He wanted to show her
everything! Then WALL•E turned on his video of *Hello, Dolly!*
He danced for EVE as the music in the movie played. He
even tried to hold her hand—like the people in the movie—
but EVE didn't understand.

WALL•E showed EVE the little green thing in the boot. That was when something strange happened. EVE zeroed in on the green thing, snatched it away, and locked it inside her. Then she shut down completely. Her only sign of life was a flashing green light on her chest.

"Eee-vah?" WALL•E tapped her timidly.

EVE didn't answer or move. It was as if she was asleep.

WALL•E tried everything to wake her up.
But it was no use.

Then, one day, the probe ship
returned to pick up EVE.
"Eee-vah!" WALL•E cried frantically.
He raced to the ship that held EVE
inside. Then he grabbed on tight
as it blasted into space.

Space was full of wonders. As EVE slept inside the ship, WALL•E got a view of Earth that he had never seen before. The stars were beautiful! WALL•E wished EVE could share the sights that swept by him. At least he was near her, and could keep following her . . . wherever she was going.

Finally, the probe ship reached its destination.
"Oooh!" WALL•E stared in awe at the massive
spaceship in front of him. It was the *Axiom,* one of the
many luxury star liners in the BnL fleet. The *Axiom*
housed a whole city full of humans. The people had
grown very lazy during their centuries in space.
Robots did everything for them.

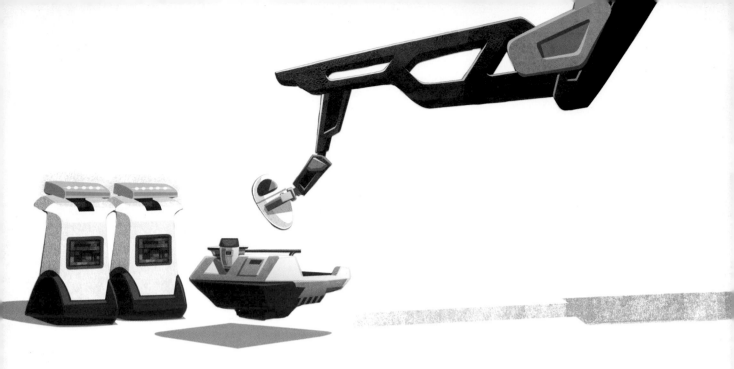

Soon WALL•E and EVE were inside the *Axiom*'s docking bay. The Captain's robot assistant, Gopher, quickly whisked EVE away. WALL•E took off after them, eager to catch up with EVE. Then a cleaner-bot named M-O joined the chase, determined to give dusty, rusty WALL•E a good scrubbing.

WALL•E raced through the *Axiom,* trying to keep up with EVE. Suddenly, a woman named Mary blocked his way. Desperate to get past her, WALL•E pulled the wires on Mary's hover chair. Her holo-screen shut off, and for the first time in her life, Mary turned her head to see the world around her. WALL•E waved happily as he moved past Mary.

WALL•E followed EVE all the way to the *Axiom*'s control
room. He hid as the Captain and his robot autopilot, Auto,
entered. Auto quickly reactivated EVE.

The Captain pressed the green light on EVE's chest. EVE woke up!

"Eee-vah!" WALL•E gasped, delighted.

"WALL•E?" Surprised, EVE motioned for him to be quiet.

Meanwhile, the Captain looked at his manual to find out what to do next.

The Captain learned that EVE's secret mission was to find signs of life on Earth. She had done that by bringing WALL•E's little green treasure—a plant—to the Captain. The living plant proved that it was safe to return to Earth!

But when the Captain eagerly opened EVE's storage compartment, it was empty. The plant was gone!

"Send her to the repair ward," the Captain ordered, pointing to EVE and sighing with disappointment. Then he spotted WALL•E. The little bot rolled up to the Captain and happily shook his hand. "And fix that robot as well. Have it hosed down or something. It's filthy."

Auto ordered Gopher to take EVE and WALL•E away.
The little cleaner-bot M-O suddenly appeared and followed,
still obsessed with scrubbing WALL•E and his dirty trail.

Broken reject-bots filled the *Axiom*'s robot repair ward. But when WALL•E saw EVE's blaster arm being removed, he thought she was being hurt. He grabbed the arm and accidentally blasted a control panel. The doors opened—and the reject-bots were free! They carried their new hero, WALL•E, out into the hallway. Suddenly, steward-bots blocked their escape route.

WALL•E and EVE were on the run!

EVE rushed WALL•E to a life pod. She wanted to send him back to Earth. Then he would be safe, and she could finish her mission. But WALL•E wouldn't leave without her. Before they could argue, someone approached.

Hiding, WALL•E and EVE watched as Gopher appeared and put something into the life pod. It was the plant! WALL•E scooted into the pod to get the plant back—just as Gopher activated the launch sequence.

Whoosh! EVE raced into space to help WALL•E.

"EEEEE!" WALL•E screamed, trying to work the pod's controls. Then he accidentally pushed the self-destruct button.

"WALL•E!" EVE screamed as the pod exploded.
Then she saw him rocketing toward her with a fire extinguisher. He had escaped—with the plant! Delighted, EVE twirled closer to WALL•E. An electric arc passed between their heads—it was a robot kiss.

From inside the ship, Mary watched WALL•E and EVE.
"Hey, look at that!" she said to John, another passenger.
She disabled his holo-screen. Blinking, John looked out
at the dancing robots. Then he smiled at Mary and
reached out and held her hand.

Back inside the ship, EVE told WALL•E to
wait for her while she delivered the plant to
the Captain. Overjoyed, the Captain held the
plant as he watched the holo-graphic images
EVE had recorded on Earth. If that plant
could survive on Earth, then so could people!

EVE watched the holo-graphic images, too.
But she saw something different. She saw
how WALL•E had tenderly cared for her while
she was shut down. And she finally
understood love.

The Captain ordered Auto to set a course
for Earth. But Auto refused. He knew that long ago,
BnL had given up on Earth. They believed it was too
polluted and would never sustain life again.

Gopher grabbed the plant and threw it over to the
trash chute. Down it went . . . then it came back up.
WALL•E had caught the plant and climbed up the chute!

The Captain was thrilled . . . until Auto zapped
WALL•E. Then both WALL•E and EVE were dropped
into the trash chute.

WALL•E and EVE tumbled down into the garbage bay. M-O tumbled down after them, still determined to clean WALL•E.

EVE desperately wanted to repair her damaged friend, but she needed parts—parts from Earth.

Now EVE had to get the *Axiom* back to Earth so that she could save WALL•E! She blasted a hole for them to escape through. Then she flew WALL•E and M-O up and out of the garbage bay.

When EVE and WALL•E
arrived at the bridge, the steward-bots
tried to stop them. Luckily, the reject-bots
began to pour into the hall to help their hero,
WALL•E. While the rejects bravely battled the stewards,
EVE flew the injured WALL•E toward a special machine
called the holo-detector.

The Captain, who had been locked in his cabin by Auto, decided it was time to take action. He tricked Auto into thinking that he had the plant. "Ha! Look what I've got, Auto!" the Captain taunted.

Auto lowered himself to the Captain's quarters to get the plant. That was when the Captain tackled him! The two battled their way back to the control room. The Captain pushed Auto aside and activated the holo-detector. Now EVE could place the plant inside the machine and finish her mission.

As soon as she saw the holo-detector, EVE raced toward it with the plant. But back on the bridge, Auto tried to lower the holo-detector. Using the last bit of energy he had, WALL•E held the machine up. Finally, the Captain stood. He flicked off Auto's power. "You are relieved of duty!" the Captain said.

EVE placed the plant in the holo-detector.
The computer scanned it and announced,
"Plant origin verified. Set course for Earth."
The *Axiom* and its passengers could go
home! EVE had completed her mission.
The holo-detector rose off WALL•E.
He fell to the floor, crushed and broken.

"WALL•E?" EVE held him close, but his power light dimmed.

EVE called his name again.

WALL•E didn't answer.

EVE knew she needed to take WALL•E back to his trailer to repair him. But would they get there in time?

Soon the *Axiom* landed on Earth.

The passengers watched as the Captain ventured out alone and knelt down in the dirt. He dug a hole and placed the plant in the ground.

Meanwhile, EVE raced the gravely damaged WALL•E to his trailer. The concerned cockroach hopped on board for the ride.

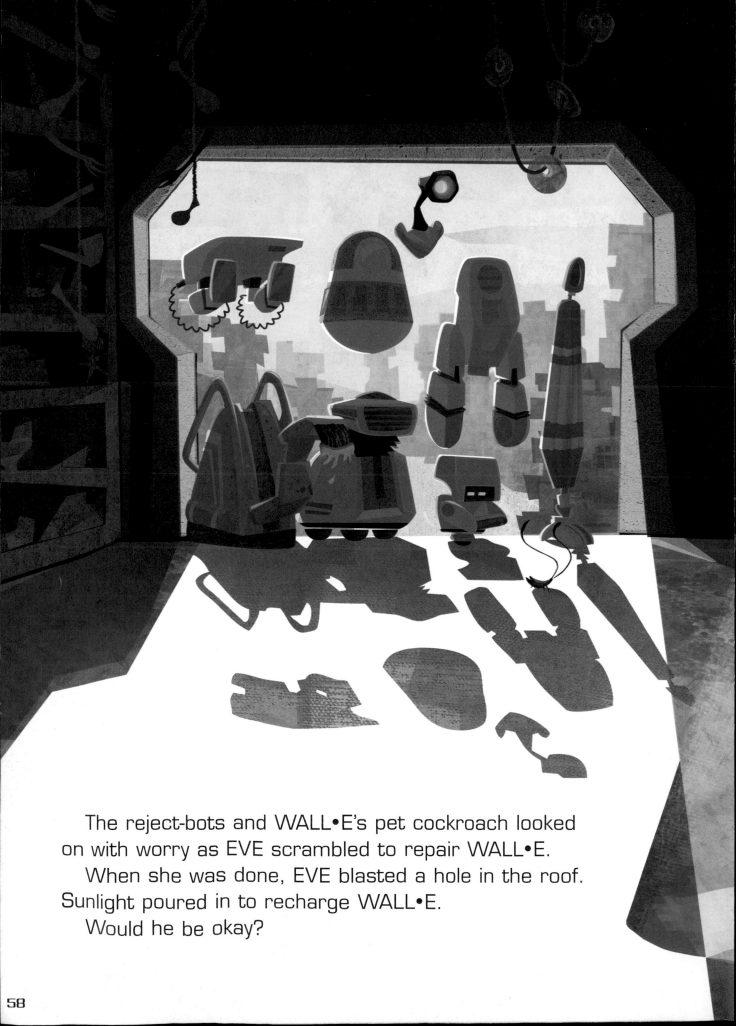

The reject-bots and WALL•E's pet cockroach looked
on with worry as EVE scrambled to repair WALL•E.
    When she was done, EVE blasted a hole in the roof.
Sunlight poured in to recharge WALL•E.
    Would he be okay?